Joy Mitchell grew up in Europe and spent most of her life studying and travelling around the world. Whilst working in the world of science during the day, she has been writing during the night, making up stories for her children.

Joy now lives on a small farm in New Zealand and writes full time. While her family members sadly refused to be written about, her trees, horses and dogs were only too happy to be featured.

Joy Mitchell

Stubs, the Stubborn Christmas Tree
Volume 1

Austin Macauley Publishers™
LONDON • CAMBRIDGE • NEW YORK • SHARJAH

A CIP catalogue record for this title is available from the British Library.

ISBN 9781528995955 (Paperback)
ISBN 9781528995962 (Hardback)
ISBN 9781528995979 (ePub e-book)

www.austinmacauley.com

First Published (2020)
Austin Macauley Publishers Ltd
25 Canada Square
Canary Wharf
London
E14 5LQ

To my mum. Thank you for always supporting me
and my wildest dreams. This one is for you!

Thank you to Kay and the whole editing team at
Austin Macauley Publishers.

Volume 1

CHAPTER 1
STUBS MEETS HIS FAMILY

It was that time of year again. Days grew shorter, the nights longer and snow started falling softly. The whole world seemed peaceful and quiet. Mama Christmas tree gathered her children again.

"Quiet, my children, quiet!" Mama Tree started to speak, "The day we have been preparing for all year is finally here. Tomorrow is the grand opening sale of Mama's Christmas trees. Like every year, I expect you all to stand tall and proud, to find a great home with a lovely family and wear the beautiful Christmas decorations with pride and honour!"

"Stubs! I see you!" Mama Tree shouted, "Come forward my little coward!" she commanded, "You are not going to hide like last year...look at you! You are much taller and unruly now than all your brothers and sisters. You will be awfully lucky if somebody wants you at all the way you look." Mama Tree shook her head in dismay.

"No, Mama. No. I want to stay here with you. I want to stay in the forest and grow to be a real tree, strong and tall...I don't want to be just a Christmas tree!" Stubs replied defiantly.

The whole place went silent, "How dare you defy our traditions?" Mama Tree was shaking with anger and needles went flying all over the place.

"We are Christmas trees and the finest in the world!" she almost shouted now, "No more of your nonsense. In fact, you will be in the front row this year! And no more talking back!"

Night fell and as the morning came, there were hundreds of people waiting outside the gates of the Christmas tree farm. There were lots of excited children with their parents, ready to take their favourite Christmas tree home.

Within the first three hours of picking, almost all trees were gone except Mama Tree (who was not for sale, as she needed to have children Christmas trees for next year of course) and Stubs, who got away from front row while Mama was not looking. Now, he was hiding in the corner of the shed and did a very good job trying to look very ugly and mis-shapen so nobody would take him away. Mama Christmas tree looked at him and let out a sad sigh.

The gardener was just about to close the gates when they heard a car screeching halt in front of the gates. It was a dirty old white pick-up truck and out came tumbling three children and three dogs.

10

The children started shouting, "We came too late, Mum! All the trees are gone! We told you, you were driving too slowly as always!"

Their pretty mum looked crushed and said softly, "I am so sorry, my darlings, maybe next year..." However, she could not finish her sentence as she saw Pebbles, one of her dogs and a huge, clumsy, black Newfoundland rushing towards the shed and starting to pee against an odd shaped wiry green thing in the corner.

"Pebbles, no – naughty dog! Come back!" Mum started to yell and ran towards the shed, but Sadie, Tim and Tom already were at Pebbles's side and pulled her away, when they happily cried out.

"Mum, it's a tree. A Christmas tree. Please, come look! Can we have him please...please?"

Mum was very surprised as she came closer, "Wow, indeed it seems to be Christmas tree. However, it seems to be a very, very strange one. Never seen anything like this before."

She turned to the gardener.

"How much is this tree? It is a Christmas tree, is it?" she asked.

"Ha, Christmas tree... Not so sure... Anyways, this one is for free. It's from last year and quite stubborn. I would not mind getting rid of him. Only causes trouble that one," the gardener responded.

"Stubborn and a troublemaker?" Mum asked. She shook her long hair and laughed, "Never heard a tree being described as stubborn. I like it. We are stubborn as well. He will fit right in."

And to Stubs greatest horror, he was bundled up and put into the back of the truck along with the three dogs Pebbles, Simba and Toto. The children climbed happily with big smiles into the car as well and so they drove home.

Having arrived at the house, Stubs was actually surprised, that the family lived in a large house in the midst of a park like garden with so many trees and overgrown shrubs. Everything looked a bit worse for the wear and neglected though. Certainly, there has not been a gardener at work for a very long time. Stubs, who was a true snob at heart, immediately decided not to like them.

They think they got themselves a treat of a Christmas tree. Ha...I will show them, that I am real tree, not some piece of greenery they can just decorate and then throw away! He thought to himself.

He gave Mum and the children a super hard time when they tried to take him off the car. He was as heavy and awkward to carry as possible. It took them one full hour to finally get Stubs to lean against a wall in the living room.

Mum was finally relaxing and clutching her back, "Wow. He was certainly a lot heavier than he looks," she said. She looked confused, "And now what do we do children? Is he not opening his branches?" They all stared at Stubs.

"I have an idea," Tim shouted, "I am sure, he is thirsty. Look, how dry he looks," and he came back with two huge pots of water and all of them helped to put Stubs trunks and roots into it and then went about the house to get changed.

Immediately, Stubs relaxed a bit. Ahh, this feels good. Finally, water again. He thought. And premium water as well, as he could always tell different waters apart and was very proud of this ability.

"Mum, look." Sadie the youngest of the children, who has been hiding in a corner, screamed and pointed at Stubs, "Look at the branches coming open... he is gorgeous Mum. Tim! Tom! You need to see this!"

Mum and the other children looked at Stubs in surprise. Sadie was right. The strange and green wiry thing had turned into the most amazingly beautiful Christmas tree. He was standing tall and straight with his green, lush branches everywhere and they almost reached the ceiling.

"Wow, we have never had such a beautiful Christmas tree," Mum said.

They children jumped up and down, "Thank you, Santa!" they squealed.

Stubs was immediately disgusted again, "Santa! Ba – the old bag. What did he have to do with my luscious branches? Nothing! Zero! NADA! Nil! It is called exercise and healthy food. Discipline and working out!"

Stubs has always prided himself in being the Christmas tree who was most disciplined. He would work his branches long after his brothers and sisters were already asleep and only put his roots in the most nourishing water. Santa-ha! I will show them... But as he wanted to grumble and shake a little bit more, he realised, he was exhausted and was asleep before finishing his thought.

In the morning, Stubs opened his eyes and wanted to start stretching as he did every morning, but he could not move. He panicked and unsure for a moment unsure where he was, he looked around. It has not been a nightmare. This was real. He was in somebody's living room, tied to the wall and covered in full Christmas decorations and lighting.

"Oh no," he shrieked horrified, "I thought, it was a bad dream. I was turned into a Christmas decoration and am stuck in some country bumpkin home. Help! Help!"

With all his might, he wiggled, struggled and finally managed to break free from the rope that tied his branches. Immediately, he started to shake all the ornaments and lights off and make them fly through the room in every direction. It was such a commotion, that the three dogs who were lying to his feet jumped up and started barking.

"What is it Toto?" Tim came running in and cradled the smallest dog. He was the youngest child, a bit short sighted and needed to find his glasses first. He looked around the living room.

"Mum come fast! Something terrible has happened!" he yelled. Mum came rushing in her pyjamas, swinging a huge frying pan ready to attack an expected intruder.

Tim pointed to their Christmas tree, "Look, all our decorations are gone-all gone," and he started crying, "Tomorrow is Christmas, and we don't even have a decorated tree."

Mum kneeled down and hugged him really tight. She looked around the destroyed living room and frowned at the awkward tree in the corner.

Stubs immediately felt very bad. Oh gully he thought... *I am so, so sorry. I really did not mean to hurt that little kid's feelings. Maybe Mama Tree was right and it is an honour to be a Christmas tree? But I want to be a real tree and be outside and free! What can I do?* Stubs started to angle for the fallen ornaments with his lower branches and tried to put them back on.

"Look Mum and Tim," Sadie and her older brother Tom, who were now awake pointed excitedly at Stubs, "It looks like our tree is trying to get the ornaments back on! He is alive!"

"Nonsense, Tom and Sadie," Mum scolded them, "There is no such thing as a living Christmas tree." However, as she turned around, she thought she caught tears falling down this most unruly of Christmas trees. She let go of Tim and got closer to Stubs to look at him properly. Immediately, Stubs froze. Oh my! What have I done now? Mama will be so mad. I can do nothing right! And to his great horror another big fat tear splashed down.

"Hey, you," all of a sudden Sadie came over and started hugging Stubs, "Don't be sad, we love you just the way you are! If you do not want to wear ornaments, that is okay. You are beautiful the way you are!" Stubs stopped crying, looked down and could not believe what he saw.

This little human hugging his branches very tight.

"His name is Stubs," Sadie said, "And he is very sad, as he wants to be a real tree in the forest and have his roots back in the earth."

Sadie's brothers laughed at her, "You and your nonsense. Trees can't talk."

Stubs held his breath. How come this little human could read his thoughts? "She must be really special."

"Sadie, Darling," Mum said, "I know you love trees and flowers, but remember, we said that they are not living things?"

"Untrue." Sadie started marching up and down, "All flowers and trees are living things."

"Maybe, but certainly not Christmas trees?" Tim asked? "Those are just decorations and get thrown out after Christmas is over...You know. It is like a thanksgiving turkey, sort of."

WHOOSH. Stubs was so mad, that he threw a stuffed teddy across the room at Tim's head, "How dare you say, I am just a decoration?"

Sadie and Tom stared laughing, "HAHA, he heard that and he does not seem to like you one bit!"

Mum let go of the frying pan and looked at Stubs more

closely. Touching his branches gently, she turned
to Sadie,
"Darling, I don't know if you really can talk to this tree.
However, I tend to agree trees and flowers are living
things and should be treated better. How about, if we
plant our stubborn Christmas tree outside in front of the
living room? We can decorate him outside and that way
we always have a Christmas tree every year? And he can
have the roots in the fresh earth and his branches
fresh air."
Sadie screamed, "Yippee! Mum, THANK you," and hugged
her and started dancing. Tom joined in, but Tim was still
furious and getting rid of Stubs needles in his sweater,
"Whatever," he mumbled.
Stubs could not believe his ears or his needles, so to
speak. He started bobbing nervously up and down, "Stop
fussing Stubs!" Sadie tried to calm him down, "Everything
will be okay now." And so, he finally relaxed and made
himself as light as possible as the family carried
him outside.
"Very weird Mum," Tim muttered, "The tree is so much
lighter and easier to carry than yesterday."
"Because he is happy to be outside of course," Sadie
explained and smiled, "And I think, he likes us now!"
Outside, Mum and the children found a beautiful soft
spot in the earth and dug a little hole. As soon as Stubs
felt his feet (aka roots) inside the earth again, he
relaxed and gave out a big sigh.
"Thank you, humans," he said and pulled mum, Sadie, Tim
and Tom into a big hug.

Mum laughed and brushed him off, "All good Stubs. I don't think. I would want to be stuck in a room with cut off feet either. I totally understand. But it is still Christmas...would you mind, if we decorate you just a little bit for the Christmas spirit?"

As Stubs nodded, the children and dogs ran inside and came towing all sorts of ornaments, ribbons and lights. This time around, Stubs stood totally still as the family decorated him and he wore his ornaments and lights with pride.

He grew to become the biggest and most beautiful Christmas tree in the whole area and visitors came from afar to see him.

Naturally, many were unsure to believe that the family could actually talk to Stubs and that the name of this amazing Christmas tree was really Stubs.

But Christmas Time is a magical time and miracles do happen, right?

CHAPTER 2
STUBS SAVES CHRISTMAS

One fine day, Stubs was bored.
He was home alone. Mum Tannenbaum was at work. The children Sadie, Tim and Tom were at school. The dogs Pebbles, Simba and Toto were at their monthly grooming day.
Stubs was looking around for things to do, maybe annoy a bird or scare a rabbit, when suddenly the sky went dark.
A loud thunder roared and immediately Stubs looked for cover. Thunder and lightning go hand in hand. Like all trees, he was much afraid of lightning, even if he did not like admitting it. But before he could hide, he heard a loud thud behind him, and the sky turned bright and calm again.
"That is so odd," Stubs thought out loud. "I have only seen this behaviour of the sky around Christmas and we are still far away from it." He turned around and froze, as he saw a huge reindeer grinning at him.
"Hey Stubs! Still talking to yourself I see."
"Donner!" Stubs screamed in surprise, "I should have thought it was you, hearing that strange thunder on a clear sky." Donner meant thunder of course and Donner was Santa's favourite reindeer.
"I have not seen you in ages! What are you doing here? Are you not a bit too early coming to earth? Christmas is in three months. Did you bring the old bag as well?"

Stubs excitedly looked around. He was so bored; he would have even been happy to talk to Santa. With old bag, he meant Santa Claus of course. Stubs did not particularly like him. This went back hundreds of years. Santa Claus and the family of Christmas trees could never agree who is more important and the one, true symbol for Christmas.

Santa said, him of course, as he is the one bringing all the presents. The Christmas trees argued, without them there would not be a place to put the presents. The gifts would be put on any odd table and that would be just another birthday. Not the special birthday of Christ. Also, the word Christmas trees of course means Christ's tree.

Santa and the reindeers disagreed, and the feud has never been solved. They must get along, but they do not really like each other. Except Donner. Stubs loved Donner and Donner loved Stubs. They would always go on fun outings when they were growing up. And always got into trouble of course. Donner was fun. Stubs looked happily at his friend.

But Donner shook his majestic head and looked sad. "No Stubs, no Santa. That is exactly why I am here. He needs your help."

Stubs almost toppled over, "Santa, needing my help. Whatever for? Please explain?"

Donner walked around nervously, "We do not have much time. Mum is on her way back with the dogs and the school bus is around the corner."

"How do you know that?" Stubs asked.

"We know everything that happens on earth, remember?" Donner smiled, "Quite a lovely family you found yourself Stubs. Incredibly lucky."

"I know, I know." Stubs got impatient, "I love them to pieces and would protect them always. Now stop stalling. What is wrong with Santa?"

24

"He broke his leg and cannot carry out Christmas presents on his own. You are the only walking Christmas tree on earth at present. You need to help." Donner looked at Stubs.

"Wow, slow down." Stubs was confused, "How can Santa break his leg? He is a celestial being, it is impossible."

"Well." Donner had hoped not having to explain and looked nervous, "We were all on holiday. You know, once a year, everybody needs a holiday." He started defensively, but Stubs interrupted, "I know, I know, I just came back from holiday with my family. Loved it. In fact, I would love to go again."

Donner continued, "Well, our holiday naturally has to be taken in summer and we all went to an amusement park, where they had a Christmas in July day. Everybody dresses up as Christmas characters, mostly Santa. And, ah... I might have been watching the wrong Santa on the 'Merry-Go-Round." Donner looked very uneasy now and dragged his hooves nervously, "And it might have been that the real Santa fell out. Since we had to be in human form for the holiday, he was able to break his leg. And his arm."

Stubs laughed out loud, "I would have loved to see that. You got into big trouble, didn't you? I assume now you want me to clean up your mess?"

"Please, please, would you?" Donner blinked excitedly, "I would owe you one."

"Just me, or my family? I want you to include my family?" Stubs asked.

"Okay, I owe you and your family." Donner sighed. He thought, he knew exactly what that meant. Stubs had always wanted to use him as a horse and Donner always objected. He was a reindeer, not a horse of course.

"Perfect," Stubs said, "We might have a deal. What do you want me to do?"

"You need to go down the chimneys at Christmas and

deliver the presents." Donner replied.

"What? Heavens no. I do not like tight spaces, you know that. Anything, but going down the chimneys." Stubs was not happy and shook his branches vigorously.

"You have to, Stubs. There will be no Christmas if you do not help. The pixies will sprinkle pixie dust and make you very small." Donner almost begged now.

Stubs walked up and down, "Donner you were always my favourite. But Santa and I do not get along. Maybe, it's not such a good idea after all."

"Please, Stubs. Santa even gave me a letter for you." Donner showed him a bright envelope now with a letter in Santa's handwriting, which said:

"Stubs, I need your help to save Christmas. Please." Signed, Santa Claus.

Stubs was silent. He did not think Santa has ever said please to anyone. He did not need to. He was the boss. That gave him an idea.

"Would that mean, I am boss for the day and you have to do what I say?"

Donner was dreading this, "Yes, unfortunately."

Stubs perked up, "Well, why did you not say so in the first place? Of course, I will help. I need to tell my family though."

"What do you need to tell me and who is your friend?"

Stubs and Donner jumped. Mum had come home and looked incredulously at this huge brown animal looking like a reindeer in her backyard.

"Mum, sorry, may I introduce my old friend Donner." Stubs pointed at the reindeer.

"Donner?" mum asked, "As in Donner and Blitzen? Santa's reindeers?"

"Yeah, yeah." Donner replied annoyed, "Why am I always mentioned in the same sentence as that goofball, no good brother of mine. Beats me. I am Donner, pleased to meet you Mum!" Donner bowed.

26

Mum laughed. Ever since Stubs joined their family, she was not really surprised about anything anymore. She was talking to a tree and a huge reindeer was looking at her expectantly.

"Lovely to meet you Donner! But are you not a bit early? Did I oversleep and it is Christmas already? Where is Santa?" she looked around.

"Funny story, Mum." Stubs laughed and Donner looked very embarrassed, "Santa broke his arm and his leg. Donner's fault. Now they need my help to save Christmas. Can I Mum, Please?" Stubs looked excited and bobbed from one root to the other.

Mum smiled. She loved this stubborn, kind-hearted Christmas tree, who brought so much joy into their lives. Now Stubs wanted her permission to help Santa Claus. THE SANTA CLAUS. How could she say no?

"Sure. Stubs and Donner go ahead help Santa save Christmas."

Stubs gave her a big hug, "Thanks Mum. You are the best. I cannot wait to tell Sadie and Tim and Tom!" And he looked out for the children.

"Wait a minute, Stubs." Mum objected, "We cannot spoil Sadie's and Tim's illusion of Santa Claus. But we can tell Tom. He can help you."

Donner was happy about this, "Mum. Stubs. I need to leave now. The children are just around the corner. Stubs, thank you. I will pick you and Tom up at Christmas Eve. Pleasure meeting you." He nodded to Mum, and amid another thunder, he raced up the roaring sky and was gone in seconds.

Sadie, Tim and Tom came running shortly after and the family had a lovely peaceful meal.

After dinner, Stubs drew Tom aside and told him everything. Tom has always been the most suspicious of the three Tannenbaum children and did not believe him at first, "Utter nonsense Stubs. Santa does not exist, how childish. And I do not believe in Donner either."

Stubs looked exasperated at the sky and yelled, "Donner! Help."

Immediately, a huge thunder roared in the sky, "okay, okay." Tom held his ears, "I believe you. What do you need me to do?"

Stubs explained, "You and I are going down the chimneys and putting presents under the trees. Since I am not as fast as Santa, you need to help."

Tom agreed but did not know what to believe. On one hand, he had a Christmas tree as a friend. On the other hand, he did not believe in Santa anymore and thought it was child's play. He went to bed that night and totally forgot about it. Until Christmas Eve.

"Mum! Tom!" A crying Sadie ran through the house and woke him up, "Stubs does not want to wear Christmas decorations this year. And he does not want to come inside." Tim cried as well.

Stubs looked sadly at Mum, who looked sadly at Sadie and Tim. In agreeing to save Christmas for the world, they messed up Christmas for their own family. But before they could start to explain, a huge thunder started to roar, and the sky went black.

"Mum, please take Sadie and Tim to the markets. Tom, we need to go. Don't worry, we will find a way to save our Christmas, I promise." Stubs grabbed Tom and Mum distracted Sadie and Tim, shooting a glance at Stubs and Tim riding up the sky on Donner.

Tom could not believe his eyes. He was riding on a reindeer into the sky. So fast, he did not dare to blink or miss anything. He would have loved the ride to be longer, but what seemed like only seconds they arrived in a small village in the clouds.

"Is this heaven?" he whispered to Stubs, completely stunned.

"Don't be silly, Tom, of course not. This is Santa Ville. The Christmas village." Stubs nudged his little friend off the reindeer. They had landed in a big square filled with brightly coloured presents. Mountains of presents.

"There you are!" Santa himself approached Stubs and Tom on crutches, "Good to see you, Stubs. I know we have not seen eye to eye the last 1000 years or so, but I am grateful that you are helping me. And you too Tom." Santa started shaking Tom's hand, "Forgive me using my left hand. My right one is still broken." Santa shot a grim look at Donner. "Now, off you go. No time to lose. The reindeers know the way, same route as every year. Oh, and I almost forgot. Pixies please come here and sprinkle dust!" Santa waved a couple of pixies over and to Tom's big surprise, he saw a dozen tiny pixies sprinkle fine golden dust onto him, and Stubs and they started to shrink. Soon, they were the size of a cat.

"Stubs. I am scared." Tom pressed close to his Christmas tree, "Don't be, my child." Santa smiled, "Once you have delivered all the presents, you will get your size back. Now go!"

All the reindeers were ready and eager to go. The presents were all loaded on the sleigh and the pixies waited on the side. Stubs and Tom climbed inside the sleigh, buckled up and the reindeers immediately took off in the sky.

Stubs was excited, "I always wanted to ride in the sleigh, but Santa never let me. Tom, do you love it?" Tom did not reply. He was silent with wonder. Stubs thought, he had never seen him so happy. As the oldest child in the family, Tom sometimes carried too much weight on his shoulder and was too serious for his age. Stubs was so pleased to see him so happy.

Soon, the sleigh arrived at the first roof and Blitzen shot up a lightning in the sky.

"This is your sign Stubs and Tom," Donner said, "Every time Blitzen shoots up a lightning, you grab the first sac. Go down the chimney, put the presents under the trees and come back up. five Second tops."

"Five seconds, Stubs." Tom woke up from his trance and was scared, "That is impossible."

"Don't worry, Tom. We have pixie dust on us, that makes us lightning fast, I show you." Stubs shouldered the first sac, took Tom's hand and raced across the roof. Going down the chimney was not as bad as Stubs has feared. He and Tom put the presents under the trees and wanted to race back up the chimney when he got side-tracked.

"Cookies, Tom. Look." He pointed to a set of cookies on a sofa table, "And the good kind with chocolate, freshly baked and warm. Now I know, why Santa has such a big belly. Have one, Tom!"

Stubs sat down on the sofa and helped himself to the cookies, "That is a mighty comfy sofa as well Tom. We might have to talk Mum into getting one like that, I love it." Stubs and Tom just made themselves comfortably when they heard a roar down the chimney. Along came Donner, all black and bruised and dusty as he did not pixie dust in time.

"Are you crazy? Stubs! Tom! You took 15 seconds already. Way overtime. You are not supposed to eat cookies and sit on the sofa every time you go to a different house!" Donner was super mad, "Stubs. You need to take this seriously, please!"

"So sorry, Donner." Stubs was honestly crushed, "I see a cookie and forget the world."

"Well, literally," Donner grumbled, as they made their way up the chimney and climbed back into the sleigh, "No more cookies or delays. We need to make up time. Children are more important than cookies."

Tom laughed, "I think, Stubs would disagree." But he stopped talking, as Stubs gave him such a shove, he almost fell out of the sleigh.

"Traitor," Stubs cried but grinned at Tom. He started to enjoy being on the sleigh with the reindeers and playing Santa.

"Please Donner, may I say it? I promise, no more silliness." Stubs looked at his friend.

"If you must." Donner smiled.

"Say what?" Tom asked, but Stubs was already swinging the whip and calling into the sky: "HOHOHO, Donner and Blitzen, Dasher and Dancer, Prancer and Vixen, Comet and Cupid, let us go!"

The reindeers all rolled their eyes and Comet hissed: "You got to be kidding me." But they all knew their duty and raced thru the sky from one chimney to the other. Stubs and Tom got faster and faster with each chimney and the night was not even over when Donner called out, "Finished! Well done everyone, all presents delivered in magical time, 2.5 celestial minutes faster than Santa, that is 2.5 hours in the human world."

Stubs hugged Tom and had an idea, "Donner, remember that you owe me a favour? I would like to call that in!"

Donner sighed, "That did not take you long, but sure, a deal is a deal, what would you like? More cookies? Me saying Stubs is the greatest?"

Stubs shook his branches, "No Donner, nothing for me, but for my family. I could not be there for my family today. We saved Christmas for the rest of the world, now please help me save Christmas for my little world."

Donner was surprised and got a little teary eyed. Stubs had really changed. The selfish, stubborn Christmas tree has become kind, loving and generous, almost human. Donner was impressed.

"That is very thoughtful of you. What do you want me to do?" Donner asked.

"Please pick Sadie, Tim, Mum and the dogs up and bring them to the Santa Village." Stubs begged his friend.

Donner replied with a frown: "I would love to help but going back to earth needs permission from Santa. We are not allowed to come and go, as we please. That would irritate and upset the human world."

Whilst they were talking, the sleigh had landed in the Christmas village and Santa walked up to them.

"Wonderful work Stubs and Tom. Well done! You both saved Christmas, thank you so very much! Now, as a thank you present each one of you can wish for whatever you want!"

Santa looked at Tom, "Tom, you go first."

Tom looked at Santa, "I want my mum and Sadie and Tim and the dogs with me to celebrate Christmas."

"Hmmm, excellent wish," Santa said, "And you Stubs?"

"Same. I want my family with me, nothing else. Please Santa. I already checked with Donner. He and the others would be happy to help."

Santa was pleased, "Wonderful wishes, thoughtful, kind and caring, true Christmas spirit. I am incredibly pleased and happy to fulfil your wishes. Donner and Blitzen, get Cupid and Comet and pick up Stubs's and Tom's family."

The reindeers took off once more and Santa turned around, "We are not done yet. Pixies, please decorate

35

Stubs! Tom, help the pixies to put the presents under the trees."

Tom was confused, "What presents? I thought we gave them all away?"

Santa laughed and snapped his finger, "Turn around Tom!"

Tom turned and could not believe his eyes. Stubs was standing in the middle of the square decorated with the brightest lights and colours and beaming with pleasure. There were hundreds of presents under his branches, big and small, square and round, all wrapped in golden and silver paper. Everything sparkled.

"Wow? How?" Tom asked.

"I am Santa Claus. There is nothing I cannot do, well except speeding up a broken leg and arm."

At that moment, the reindeers landed the Santa Sleigh again at the Square. Santa shot a look at Donner and smiled. His favourite, impossible reindeer had outdone himself. He was pleased.

Sadie, and Tim jumped out of the sleigh, before it came to a full stop and Mum had trouble controlling the excited dogs.

The whole family stood in front of Stubs and the presents and could not believe their eyes.

Stubs was radiant and happy. The children glowing and smiling and Mum so happy, her heart was bursting with joy.

"This is the best Christmas ever!" The children screamed.

"The best Christmas ever!" Stubs and Donner agreed happily. And even the other reindeers nodded their heads.

Santa watched all of them and smiled. The Best Christmas ever, indeed.

All was well in the world. At least tonight.

CHAPTER 3
STUBS GETS LOST IN NEW YORK AND MEETS THE NUTCRACKER

One fine day, Stubs was bored again. Bored and Cranky. Christmas was coming up; his favourite time of the year and he was going to be alone. ALONE. AT CHRISTMAS. Him, Stubs, the personified symbol of Christmas. He sniffed. Not fair, his family abandoning him. Not fair at all.

Mum Tannenbaum, who was a geologist, was invited to go to New York for Christmas to give a talk about some boring stones she found. Stones! Bah. Boring.

What good are stones? They just lay there and do nothing. Nothing at all. They cannot even talk. Like him, or walk, like him. Mum should be talking about him, yes, she should.

And to make it worse, Mum was taking the children Sadie, Tim and Tom with her. They were all invited to stay in a fancy hotel and Mum said, it will be the chance of a lifetime and she cannot refuse.

Snubs sniffed again, watching his family through the window. They were all happily packing and chatting away. Not a soul thinking about him. He sniffed again and a big tear drop splashed down. And another one. And before he knew it, Stubs was crying for the first time.

"Mum." Sadie cried, "Something is wrong with Stubs. Come fast." And she ran outside as fast as she could. "Stubs. What is wrong? Are you sick? What is all that greasy slimy stuff coming off you?"

Sadie tried to touch it but jumped away. That stuff was seriously glibbery and sticky. But since she loved Stubs with all her heart, she gave him a hug anyway. Which made Stubs cry even more.

"Whoooaao…" Stubs continued to wail.

"I am not sick; I am crying Sadie. Well maybe, I am heart

sick." He hugged his human friend with all his mighty branches.

"What is wrong, Stubs?" Mum had arrived trying not to laugh at the picture of her daughter and her Christmas entangled in green branches and slimy stuff.

"I am crying, Mum. And I see that smirk. Normally, we Christmas Trees out of the oldest and most worthy generations of Christmas Trees do not cry, as it is undignified." Stubs sniffed again.

"But this is a special circumstance. How do you not understand?" Stubs and Sadie looked at Mum sternly.

"What are you talking about Stubs?" Mum was unsure. Tim, who had run outside as well asked:

"Did Pebbles get into your stash of chocolate cookies?" and Tom said: "Did you watch another episode of that sad show about bacteria and trees? We told you not to do that."

"Papperlapp. This is beyond cookies and TV." Stubs brushed himself off and made himself as tall as possible. "I cannot believe you do not realise what you are doing to me. ABANDONMENT. Yes ABANDONMENT. You are leaving me ALONE, on Christmas! It is not fair at all. Christmas is my time, our time!"

Mum, Sadie, Tim and Tom understood now, and they looked at each other horrified. Even the dogs Pebbles, Simba and Toto let their heads hang.

In all their excitement about getting the offer to come to New York to give a speech, they had indeed forgotten Stubs.

"So sorry, Stubs. I forgot it is Christmas. I forgot to ask if I could take you." Mum apologised softly.

"Forgetting Christmas? Forgetting Me?" Stubs was almost hysterical now and had to sit down.

"Mum. Can't we take Stubs with us? Please? I won't go without him." Sadie sat down next to Stubs and gave him a hug.

39

"Yes, Mum. Please. We won't go either." Tim and Tom sat on the other side of Stubs and gave him a hug too. Mum smiled looking at her children surrounding this most impossible of Christmas trees and all looking very feisty. "Stubs. Children. I am deeply sorry I forgot Stubs. Stubs you are right; you are family and a family should be together for Christmas." she sat down as well and crinkled her nose.

"But how are we going to get you on that plane? And what will you do whilst we are in New York sightseeing?"
Stubs jumped up all excited now and danced around waving his branches.
"I have an idea! I have a great idea! You are all going on the plane tomorrow and I will ask Donner to fly me to New York and we will meet up there."
The children got all excited now as well and danced around with him.
"What a perfect Christmas this will be!" Tom said
"What a perfect Christmas this will be in New York!" Tim cried
"What a perfect Christmas this will be in New York with Stubs!" Sadie shouted
"Perfect. Yes. I hope." Mum was not so convinced. Her idea of a perfect Christmas in New York had involved lot's of bubble baths, shopping trips and going to museums and the ballet. Now she had an impossible Christmas tree in tow. Stubs was hard to keep out of trouble in their own back yard, what kind of trouble might he get into in one of the biggest cities in the world? She sighed. Family is family, he was right.
"One thing though, children and Stubs." Mum looked stern now, "Remember, I got us all tickets to the Ballet to see The Nutcracker? We are still going, but Stubs must stay in the hotel room. There is no way I am going to make a spectacle trying to fit a Christmas tree in a theatre seat. Stubs? Do I have your word?"
"But Mum? Nutcracker is my favourite ballet? Are you sure...?" Stubs wanted to object but stopped talking as Mum looked mad now.
"Another word from you and you are not coming!"
"Yes, Mum, anything you say, Mum. I will see Nutcracker another time I am sure."
Stubs was super happy, and nothing could change that.
"What about me?" Louise, the hippo, who has lived with

the Tannenbaums ever since their African adventure, had woken up and waddled towards the family. Louise loved her sleep, but she was even more curious, why the whole family would stand around in the middle of the garden and has heard that last bit.

"Did you forget about me? I want to come too and have fun in New York? I am family too." Louise looked from one to the other until they started laughing.

"Louise," Mum laughed, "As much as we love you, I think a hippo walking through the streets of New York would get us thrown into the news, the zoo or worse places. But we will bring you a present."

"Maybe a bigger pool?" Louise looked hopeful, "The swimming pool is getting an itsy bit tight."

"Maybe." Mum grinned, "I see, what I can do." And she clapped her hands.

"Now off to bed children. We have an early start tomorrow to catch the plane. Stubs make sure Donner drops you in a place where a Christmas tree would not look suspicious. We better think about that now. Any ideas?" Mum looked around at the blank faces of her children and Stubs and laughed.

"I guess not," she thought out loud, "So, let me think. I remember, there is a Christmas tree farm that sells trees right in midtown which is close to our Hotel. I think a Christmas tree lot is the best place to hide a Christmas tree."

She looked at Stubs, who sort of shrugged his shoulder, "If I must, I must. I am sure, I will know not know anybody there and they probably cannot even speak to me. They might think I am a weirdo or not think at all. But anything to spend Christmas with you. You just need to promise to pick me right up."

"Yes, Mum." Sadie did not like this idea at all.

"How can we make sure, that Stubs does not get taken home by another family?"

Mum laughed, "I am sure Stubs will have no trouble being his most obnoxious, stubborn self again and refuse to go with anybody, right Stubs?" Tim and Tom grinned at how embarrassed Stubs looked now.

"Mum, I do swear, I did not know that you all were special and could talk to me and I did apologise so many times for my initial behaviour..." Stubs got all flustered, but Mum interrupted.

"I am just pulling your leg, I mean branch, Stubs. We would not miss any second with you. You might want to lay off the cookies and the special vitamin water though, just in case."

Secretly, even Mum was a bit worried another family would take her tree. Stubs indeed looked spectacular at present. He had grown to become tall and shiny with lush branches all around.

She shook off her worries though. It will be fine. Stubs was family. They belonged together. Nothing will happen. She clapped her hands again.

"Children, off to bed now! We have an early start to get to the airport. Stubs, have a great flight with Donner and say hello to him!"

And so, they went to bed and once the lights were off and the whole house and gardens were quiet, Stubs called Donner.

Donner was one of Santa's reindeers and Stubs best friend. Well best friend beside Sadie, Tim, and Tom. Donner was Stub's first best friend he should say. They have known each other for hundreds of years and got in much trouble together as well. But Donner was not all too pleased to hear from Stubs currently.

"Stubs! What is it? This is the busiest time of year and we are flat out." Donner descended with a whoosh that sounded a bit like Donner without lightning and more like a small storm.

"Seriously Donner, when will you learn to land without

making so much wind?" Stubs coughed up dust, "They should have called you Storm and not Donner!" But Stubs was all smiles and Donner too.

They really were the best of friends.

"Get to it, Stubs." Donner snarled with his hooves, "I need to go to New York tonight to make sure all presents are ready. New York is huge, you should remember from the last time you played Santa." Donner grinned now. The memory of Stubs squeezing thru chimneys was very funny.

"Funny, you should mention New York." Stubs was pleased, "I need a ride there."

"What? Are you crazy?" Donner exploded.

"Do I look like a 1-2-fly-a-reindeer service? Or one, two, three, four, five, six, seven, Donner fly me to heaven? And why anyway? What do I get out of it?"

Donner stomped, but grinned. He could not stay mad for long at his best friend, who quickly explained:

"Mum and the children are going to New York for Christmas and naturally I need to come as we are family. I would owe you one. You might need my help again sometime. You know, you might lose Santa again or such." Stub discreetly looked down. Losing Santa was a dark page in Donner's book and indeed it was Stubs, who helped him out and saved Christmas.

"You will hold that over me the rest of your life, won't you?" Donner said, "But I get it. It is Christmas and Christmas is about family. But we need to go right now. Jump up and hold on tight. It's a bit far and I am in hurry." And with that they made their way up to the dark sky in a roll of thunder and storm clouds.

Within what seemed only seconds, they were approaching New York. Millions of lights sparkled wherever you looked. Donner could never get enough of the first look at New York at night.

It was not Stubs first time to New York, but he was in awe again, "Wow Donner, what a view. I could never get tired of this. But, I mean, I do not see any trees. Will I stick out like a green thumb?" He got scared suddenly.

"Don't worry Stubs, I will drop you at an area in midtown that is reserved for the Christmas Tree farms. New York is the best place to be for Christmas and loves the Christmas Spirit. You will be just one of many trees believe me. Call me when in trouble. But not the next two days, it is Christmas Eve. I am busy. Santa would literally kill me. Got to go, Merry Christmas and have fun my friend."

And with that Donner basically threw Stubs off his back and onto an area that looked a bit like a parking lot and was filled with hundreds of Christmas trees.

Stubs picked a spot at the far end and wedged himself between two bigger trees. And after trying to make friendly conversation with the tree next to him, but got no response, he immediately went to sleep.

The next day, he woke up to unfamiliar noise. A lot of noise. Cars. Honking. Sirens. People talking. Stubs grumbled until he realised where he was. New York! Christmas! And his family is flying in today and should pick him up by tonight.

He looked around and the gates opened, and a steady stream of people flocked in. It was Christmas Eve, and everybody was in a frenzy taking a tree home. The lot cleared out fast and Stubs was finding it harder and harder to hide and fight off people.

"Mum. Dad. I want this Christmas tree." Stubs found himself being pulled by a tall boy with an obnoxiously high voice, "Mum, Dad I want this one."

"Brian, calm down." An elegant lady came around, "This tree is too small; we need a bigger and more expensive one."

"Okay, Mum," Brian grumbled, "Maybe, it is too shabby, and it does not even have a price tag. I want the most expensive tree. Not a free one." And they turned and left.

Stubs was mad. Dare them to call him shabby. He was just trying to stay under the radar and had not extended his branches. He looked around and saw the gates were closing. Thank goodness. Time to exhale and extend his branches and look for some water.

Stubs relaxed and extended all his branches and stood in all his glory right in the middle of the lot now. He had just closed his eyes for a tiny bit and did not see a huge luxury car coming into the back entrance. To his horror, Stubs suddenly felt several strong hands tearing at him putting him down and he felt a net being pulled over him.

"Wow, this is it. This is our tree. It is spectacular. Exactly, what we were trying to find. Thanks, Graham, for calling us." A dark and kind sounding voice started to speak.

Stubs was panicking. No, this cannot be happening. How is his family going to find him now? Where will they take him? He struggled and kicked on all sides as hard as he could.

"Gosh, what a heavy tree. Never seen one struggle like this. Graham give us a hand," a dark voice said sounding kind.

"Yes, Lord Sinclair. Of course, Sir. You will be happy with this tree. It will look fantastic on stage."
Another older voice mumbled.

Stage? Stubs struggled even more, but being jetlagged and tired and thirsty, he was quickly overpowered and lifted onto the luxury car.

"Where did you get this tree from anyway, Graham? I think I want one like this every year!" Lord Sinclair asked.

"Sir, to be honest, I don't know. It was just there. Like Magic." Graham scratched his head bewildered. He had no idea where it came from and could have sworn this tree was not in his lot yesterday when he closed up. And looking at him all tied up he felt bad too. The tree looked so sad. The old salesman shook his head. Nonsense. No such thing as a sad tree. Too much eggnog and potatoes probably.

Lord Sinclair echoed his thoughts.

"Magic? Nonsense, Graham. But never mind. Merry Christmas and come to the grand opening of the Nutcracker! It will be spectacular as always!" Lord Sinclair closed the car door and drove away.

Hah, the Nutcracker! Stage talk. Stubs was an inch hopeful again. He remembered Mum talking about tickets to the Nutcracker. Maybe there is hope. And with this thought and being so tired and jetlagged, Stubs fell asleep.

"Mum. Please, let us get Stubs." Sadie pushed away her chair at the breakfast table. The Family had arrived the night before and immediately went to the Christmas tree lot but found it locked.

Mum promised to be there as soon as they re-opened, but they all had overslept a little and woke up starving. Now they all enjoyed a sumptuous breakfast but were getting nervous.

"Yes, Mum, please let us go. I am sure Stubs is scared being all alone," Tim said. And Tom was already out the door, "I will get us a taxi, hurry up!" And he hailed yellow cab.

In the best of moods, they arrived at the Christmas tree lot with a huge bag of Stubs favourite chocolate cookies. Sadie, Tim and Tom could hardly wait to see Stubs again and ran from one tree to the other calling his name. But they could not find him. They looked for hours but in vain.

"Mum, so many trees, they all look alike, but no tree is Stubs." Sadie was close to tears.

"Where is he, Mum?" Tim was exhausted too. Mum looked around unhappy not knowing what to do and say.

"I have an idea." Tom walked up to the grumpy old man who sold the trees, "Sir, did you sell a tree that looked like it did not belong here? Like the tree was different?"

50

"Nonsense boy!" The old man huffed, "All trees are the same. They all came from the same forest and are all Christmas trees. If you cannot find what you are looking for, please leave. You are scaring my customers looking all gloomy and teary. That's bad for business." And he ushered them out.

But Graham was horrified. He knew, there was something about that tree he had just sold to Lord Sinclair. He had no idea how this family and the strange tree belonged together, and he would clearly not tell them, or he might have to give the money back.

Mum and the children walked back to the hotel heart broken.

"We lost Stubs." Sadie cried all the way.

"We lost our best friend." Tim was all teary eyed.

"We need to find him." Tom as the oldest tried to stay strong but was fighting tears as well. Stubs has become a beloved member of the family, they needed to find him.

"Mum, we will get him back, right?" He asked.

"Of course, we will, children" Mum replied more hopeful than she felt.

They were in New York. New Yorkers take Christmas very seriously. There were trees everywhere, in every house, in every shop window, in every public place. He could be anywhere.

But he was Stubs and he was family. And family belonged together. It was Christmas, magical things happen at Christmas. Mum turned to the children.

"Children, we will find him. I promise. It is Christmas and we will be together. But tonight, we have tickets for Nutcracker, and we need to get ready. Please."

Meanwhile, Stubs had woken up to find himself on a big theatre stage. He was a bit disorientated at first. Bright lights were shining and there was an air of festivity. The whole theatre was in full Christmas decoration, he heard violins playing and even smelled roasted chestnuts. Stubs got a huge fright and shuddered. No way! Maybe they took him to heaven? He did not want to go to heaven. Heaven is boring. Everybody behaves well in heaven. No fun. He wanted his family and go home. Stubs turned and wanted to walk off but found himself tied up against the wall. He was free with is upper branches but tightly bound at his lower legs

No chance to flee. Worse, he was fully decorated. Now he remembered. Nutcracker. Stage. Of course. They had decorated him as Christmas Tree for the Ballet. At least, they had had the decency and put him in a bucket full of nice water. Mmm, nice water too, perfect temperature. Stubs was happy but needed to focus. His family was coming to the opening night in a couple of hours and he needed to attract their attention. He was looking around. He always liked the theatre and thought of himself as highly educated. Right now, he was humming along to the music. Oh, how he loved Tchaikovsky! This might not be so bad after all, a couple of hours at the ballet.

"Look at this tree, Lord Sinclair!" One of the ballerinas pointed to Stubs, "He is moving his branches with the music and seems to enjoy it, is this a trick? Well done!" And she ran off.

"Don't be ridiculous, Vanessa." Lord Sinclair came over and looked closely at Stubs, who froze and tried to remain very still.

Indeed, there was something incredibly special with this tree. Lord Sinclair did not know what to make of it. He clapped his hands.

"Everybody, backstage! Ten Minutes to Curtain." Stubs was getting excited and started to scan the people that were flocking in. One by one, dressed up families took their seats and chatted excitingly. But Stubs lost his spirit, as he did not see his family. Maybe they missed the plane?

The curtain was raised, and the performance started. Stubs was ready to cry, as he heard commotion from the front seats. He saw Mum, Sadie, Tim and Tom sneak in and sit in the front row. His heart made a jump looking at their sad faces. Oh my, Sadie looked like she cried for hours. Tim and Tom looked gloomy and Mum's make up was all messy.

They must have been looking for him and being devastated to not find him. He must think of something quick. He did not want his family unhappy. But he could not disrupt the performance either.

Stubs looked around. This was called the Nutcracker. He was sure, he could attract attention by giving that wooden Nutcracker a shove. It was right below his branches and scratching him anyway.

He shoved as hard as he could. Whoosh, the Nutcracker landed in the middle of the stage and almost tripped up the Ballerina. A gasp went thru the audience, but his family did not look up. Hmm, maybe that was too subtle, Stubs thought and threw one of his ornaments as far as possible. It landed straight inside the oboe which made a shrieking sound and scared the drummer. The audience started to giggle.

Sadie looked up. It was not supposed to be a funny play was it? She had not watched the performance so far, being too sad looking at a Christmas tree that was not Stubs, but now she looked up. What was this?

Sadie turned to Mum and noticed she was watching the big Christmas tree that was standing in the corner intently. Now he threw candy canes at the dancing mice. "Mum. Is that Stubs?" she pulled Tim's leave excitedly, "Tim, stop crying. I think, that is Stubs."

54

Tim immediately laughed, "Yes, you are right. Stubs hates mice. Even fake ones. I think he wants to attract our attention."

Tom got his binoculars, "I don't know. He looks so big. Are you sure?"

Sadie hopped up and down the seat, "Let's wait for the break and check." And she waved to Stubs.

Stubs heart made a big jump! His family was here! And they recognised him. All will be okay. He wanted to give a little wave back, but forgot he was tied up and fell face first onto stage.

"Ohhh." The audience gasped and the music stopped. Luckily, nobody got hurt.

The children did not know what to do, but Mum jumped up onto the stage and helped Stubs back up. She whispered to Stubs, "We know, it is you. Do not worry. We will get you after the performance. Stay calm!"

And she turned to the audience, "Dear Audience. My name is Dr Amelia Tannenbaum. I am a geologist and we have brought our Christmas Tree on loan to the Ballet for this performance. I do apologise, he is still jetlagged and a bit on the clumsy side and everything will be okay from now on."

Mum bowed and left the stage. Lord Sinclair could not believe what he saw and heard but ushered the ballerinas back in.

Stubs was so proud of his family, he stood perfectly still and as upright as he could throughout rest of the performance, and everything went smoothly.

The children could hardly wait until all people had left the theatre and ran up the stage.

"Stubs. Stubs. Finally, we missed you so much. We were so worried." They all shouted on top of each other.

"Easy children." Stubs coughed happily, "You are squeezing me, I can't breathe."

Mum, Sadie, Tim and Tom were hugging Stubs so hard and

laughed and cried at the same time.

They did not even hear Lord Sinclair coming up, "Hmm. could somebody please explain what is going on?"

Mum smiled, "Believe me, sir, that you would not believe me if I told you the full story. But this tree is our tree and we need him back. I am happy to pay you back whatever you paid for him."

Lord Sinclair looked at the children, who looked at him expectantly. And he also could have sworn this most impossible of Christmas trees looked right at him too.

"No problem, you are all clearly a family and who would I be to keep a family apart at Christmas. However, could I ask a favour?"

"Anything!" Mum, Tim, Tom, Sadie and Stubs shouted at the same time.

"Can I keep your tree on loan for our performance? I will put you up in a hotel of your choice and fly you back after the season is finished in two weeks? We had raving reviews and most of them were about your tree. We sold out for all our shows. Everybody wants to have a look at this most unusual of Christmas Trees. Do we have a deal? Please?"

Mum and the children looked towards Stubs, who nodded happily and started to dance.

Lord Sinclair laughed, "I don't speak tree and I am not sure how you get him to dance but it seems like a yes to me?"

"Yes," Mum said happily, "It is a yes. Thank you so much."

The weeks flew by and they had the best of times. Mum and the children got to do all the sights and museums during the day, whilst Stubs was rehearsing with the team. And every night they sat front row watching the performance and then took him home to the lovely luxury hotel.

The last day of the season came and went fast. Stubs was bowing a last time and the audience gave them 10 curtains. Now the family rested one last night before flying home.

"Mmm, Mum, I could get used to this." Stubs was swinging in a rocking chair on the terrace of their suite and watched the lights of the city.

Sadie sniggered, "Stubs, you are famous like a rock star now. Are you sure you want to come back with us to our country bumpkin life?"

"Yes, Stubs, are you sure you can live life without personal assistants again?" Tim asked.

And Tom said: "And a life without the famous New York Hot Dogs you got so fond off?"

Stubs sighed, "Oh well, if I must, I must."

But he smiled and pulled his family into a big hug, "Home is where the heart is, and my heart is with you always. But one more Hot Dog please at Central Park?"

And so, Stubs, Mum, Sadie, Tim and Tom spent their last evening in New York sitting on a bench at Central Park eating hot dogs and watching people ice skating. And they all agreed, it had been a truly magical Christmas.

All was well in the world, at least tonight.

THE END